Desert Angels

Desert Angels

Lyman Ditson

Illustrations by Jonathan Brown, www.inkstains.com, 2022
Cover Image © CK Sandberg 2022 used by permission

Contents

Angel 1

I was just taking a short walk like I usually do. My small terrier, Lion, and I were out walking in the New Mexico desert behind my home. We were hiking through the scrub and small trees when we came upon him.

He was seated in a wooden chair behind a small folding card table. There were piles of papers about the table held in place with rocks. The desert can be windy.

He was bald and wearing a long white robe that looked a bit worn. But what really caught Lion's and my attention were the large, glowing, white wings rising from behind his shoulders. He was hunched over the table, scribbling on a sheet of paper; oddly, his wings would occasionally twitch.

I froze. What was this? Lion and I stared for what must have been two or three minutes and then suddenly the winged figure spoke without looking up, "My name Boris," he said in a thick Slavic accent.

"My name...." I stammered.

"I know you," he said as he looked up from his work, "and I know your little friend too," nodding towards Lion.

I said nothing.

He went back to his writing for a few moments. Then he spoke to us a little calmer, "You are having...how you say.... angel vision."

I was quiet. This was perplexing. An angelic vision? On one hand, this was not what I expected an angel to look like. From the bald head to the tarnished robe, to his sitting behind a card table and all his papers, it seemed a little less than divine. On the other hand, those wings on his back were the real thing. They were alive and seemed to move with his words.

But in the middle of the desert? Who would carry a card table with a chair and all these papers out here to the middle of the desert? There was nobody around except he and I and of course, little Lion.

He continued, "You think all angels the same? You think all angels pretty and perfect? Well, you wrong. Angels everywhere and some good and some not good."

Maybe he really was an angel. There was really no other explanation. But what was he doing here with me? I decided to see where this was headed.

"Why me?"

"Why me...." he whispered as he continued with his head looking down at his papers while rapidly writing. "Do you ask stars, why me? I don't know why you," he continued, "I do what told to do. That my job....and I like job."

I listened.

"They say you, so I come to you." Then he stopped writing and looked at me. "You no want angel vision?"

I was surprised by this question. Was this an angelic vision? I suppose anyone would want a vision from beyond. But I'm not sure everyone would want a vision of an angel like this.

"Uh...yes...I guess."

He folded his arms, cocked his head, and narrowed his eyes, "You not want sacred mission?"

"Sacred what?" I said not understanding.

"Mission." He went back to writing.

"What?"

"Mission..." he murmured impatiently, "mission...mission...mission."

"What mission?" I raised my voice a bit impatiently myself.

"Begin mission on ship," he answered as he went back to writing, "buccaneer ship.".

He continued a bit calmer now, "You go to ship and learn.... find captain...talk...then continue mission."

"We are in the desert," I answered, "There are no ships out here."

He raised his head and chuckled. His wings flapped with his laugh causing Lion to back up a bit.

"Maybe you have a dream, desert man...."

I wondered if this was really happening.

"This happening alright. No tricks," he said.

I stood perfectly still. What if this WAS real? What if this really was a mission from an angel?

He stopped smiling, "You write poems?" he asked.

"No. I don't write poems."

"You sure?"

"Yes, I'm sure. Why do you ask?"

Boris grinned and moved toward one pile of papers. He shuffled through them and finding the one he wanted, he held it up in front of himself.

Then he read:

Today at school I saw you
I wanted to talk to you too
You glow like the sun to me
I like you so you see

He looked at me and continued smiling. It sounded like a child's poem to me. I certainly didn't write it. And why was Boris the angel grinning like that? And then it struck me.

I DID write that. I must have been 5 years old and had a kindergarten crush. I don't even remember the name of my poem's recipient. I placed the poem on the doorstep and rang the doorbell, and then ran and hid in some bushes and watched. The target of my affection came out, looked around, picked up the paper, and disappeared back into the house.

I don't remember what happened after that. I just know I was disappointed.

"I wrote that," I said meekly.

The angel looked back down and sorted through more papers. He picked up another pile of papers and hunted through it. When he found what he was looking for, he again read from it:

Spirit is all that we are,
All things near and far,
Spirit, the boundless sky,
Where clouds slowly fly,
With all the sacred love,
From grace up above.

Again, Boris looked up at me. This poem struck a bell. But where had I heard it before? And yet my mind seemed empty as I tried to remember. And again, like a lightning bolt from the sky, I remembered.

"I wrote that in 4th grade for extra credit. The teacher made me read it in front of the class."

I stopped. It shook me as I remembered being mocked and hit with paper balls on the way back to my seat those many years ago. I was the laughingstock of the class all year after that. Now, briefly, I felt the hurt that I had undergone back then.

"Oh my God," I whispered.

Boris picked up a paper off the table and again began reading:

A soldier I am in blue,
to perform my duty true,
These lands safe to keep,
So others can soundly sleep.

This one I remembered right away. It was a poem I had written many years ago as a soldier. It had been published in a military magazine. But that wasn't the end of it. One of the other soldiers in my unit came across the poem and everyone in my unit had seen it before long. Again, I was the laughingstock of seemingly everyone.

I looked down at the ground.

The angel, Boris was on to something. I had written some poems decades ago. But they were all experiences that I had forced myself to forget. And why was Boris asking me about this now? I looked up.

He was gone. The disheveled angel had disappeared along with his card table and all his papers.

At that moment a gentle wisp of wind brushed my face.

I sat down, cross-legged, and tried to gather myself. Confused, I held my head in my hands and closed my eyes. What just happened?

I couldn't very well tell others about my desert experience. They wouldn't believe me. Nuts, even I had a hard time believing myself.

Enlightenment

I walked up to a squirrel and pointed
to the stars overhead shining in the darkness of night.
I said,
"Those are called stars."

I smiled at the squirrel and pointed
to an oak whose trunk was twisted in the nearby earth.
I said,
"That is called a tree."

Next, I showed the squirrel the timepiece
on my wrist that glimmered in the bright moonbeams.
I said,
"This is called a watch."

I was so proud of myself for teaching
this squirrel about the universe in which we both lived.
I said,
"Now you understand these things."

He then looked up at me with little black eyes
as I waited for any questions he might have.
The squirrel said
nothing and hopped away.

Angel 2

I opened my eyes, or I thought I opened my eyes.

I was sitting at the bow of a ship. I looked down at my dog, Lion. He seemed as surprised as I was. Was I dreaming? I pinched the back of my hand. It hurt. I closed my eyes again and opened them. I was still on the ship. It seemed real enough. If I was dreaming, I could do things by choice as if I were awake.

I stood up.

The ship was a wooden ship from the 1800s, I guessed. It was about 100 feet long and had masts with huge, billowing sails. It was sailing through the water fast and I could feel the wind on my face. Lion and I, for some reason, were at the narrow prow of this ship looking forward over the sea.

"Quack, quack."

I looked around. Where did that come from?

"Quack, quack."

I looked to the side next to me and grasping the edge of an open barrel was a large green parrot. He appeared to be squinting at me.

"Quack, quack."

"Quack," I answered back.

"I'm sorry," said the parrot, "I don't speak duck very well."

"Nor do I," I answered.

He leaned forward, "You are a duck, aren't you?"

"I most certainly am not," I retorted.

"Oh, sorry."

He glanced around the deck of the ship.

"My eyes aren't so great.... need to get some concentrated carrot pills...hmmm?"

He stuck his head in the barrel and seemed to be moving things around. I thought for a moment about suggesting glasses for his sight, but I dismissed the idea as the parrot had no ears on which to hang the glasses.

"Oh dear, I wish I could find them," he echoed.

"Aha!" his head popped up and in his beak was a large oblong orange pill. He promptly raised his head and gulped down the pill. He then looked out over the ocean from the bow.

"Looks all clear ahead."

I looked forward to the horizon and saw dark clouds. No

doubt a storm lay straight ahead; although it was a distance away, it still looked ominous.

"I don't know about that.... doesn't look so good to me."

"Hmmm," he said as he buried his head back in the barrel, "need more carrot pills."

His head popped up and he gulped down another orange pill. He turned his head towards me, "Would you like a carrot pill? Or perhaps a Vitamin T pill?"

"...good for your brain," he added.

"No thanks," I said.

"You know," he said matter-of-factly as he looked forward again, "it's not easy being captain of a ship. You must be on your toes...err...claws I mean. You have to navigate by the stars and keep vigilant of where you're headed."

"Where are you headed?" I asked.

"To a very special place," he answered as he leaned into the wind, "on a remote island."

"It's there that the Tree of Eternity exists," he spoke, squinting at the horizon.

"Tree of Eternity?"

"Yes. Just touch the tree and you can live forever, or at least a thousand years."

I looked at him a bit bewildered as he paused. Then he spoke again.

"All my life I have been eating vitamins and drinking juices. I have studied the science of the body and talked with renowned scientists. Yet still, nobody has reached the goal of the body living forever."

The sails were full, and the ship swiftly cut through the water.

He turned his head and looked at me again, "How about a spinach lozenge?"

"Not right now," I answered.

Then there were no sounds except the spray of the sea. After a thoughtful minute, I spoke.

"You can't live forever you know. Eventually, something will happen." Like a storm, I thought.

"Nonsense!" he said, "These are special times we live in. Anything is possible!"

At that moment, I felt sorry for this misguided parrot. All his energy was devoted to immortality. And it wasn't going to work.

I paused for a second and then asked, "Where exactly is this island?"

"I'm not positive but I think the island is straight ahead."

"When was the last time you saw a map of it?"

"I can't remember," he said thoughtfully. He then lowered his head into the barrel and began foraging for pills again. "Let's see...vitamin T...vitamin T...need...to...find ...some...vitamin T," his voice echoed.

This was pointless and a bit odd, but no odder than my desert experience with Boris had been. I then closed my eyes and, after a moment, opened them again.

I was back in the desert.

I felt a twinge of guilt. I felt like I was abandoning the poor parrot and any other souls who might have been aboard the ship. I wasn't sure the parrot really knew where he was going.

But there was something else. I was back in the desert all right, but none of the landscape looked familiar to me. Where was I?

Birth of a Universe

From the stillness
of an eternal ocean,
a great wind rises up
and screams at the silence.

A rebel is born
who calls forth the seeds of
mortal creation
and destruction.

And in the guise of virtue,
spins illusions
of a flawless
future.

But the ageless waters
wait in silence for the
insurgent spirit
to fade.

And after all motion passes,
the ripples disappear
off the surface
of the timeless.

Angel 3

I decided to head back home. The only problem was that I was lost. It struck me as funny, as the parrot I had just met also seemed to have been lost. I walked through the scrub bushes for a few minutes and had the feeling that somebody was watching me. I stopped.

Suddenly I heard the sound of wings flapping and a shadow passed over me. A moment later, a tall vulture landed in front of me. I felt a wave of fear as he was indeed a large bird and had a rather nasty-looking beak. His head was red and bare and he was covered with dark feathers. He cocked his head, studied me, and then spoke with a creaky voice, "Are you looking for a tomb?"

I was startled.

"Tomb?" I spoke, "Me?"

"Yes," he said, "a tomb for when your body comes back to life."

This made me very uncomfortable.

"Follow me," he said "I'll show you. There's nothing to be afraid of."

He hopped a short distance away, then turned and waved his wing for me to follow.

I started to follow him. Why, I wasn't sure.

He hopped with his wings spread out. I followed him for roughly half an hour as he led me to a mountain about a quarter of a mile away. Then I began to tire.

Soon we reached the small mountain. We began the climb up with him hopping and me following about 20 yards behind, exhausted. Finally, he stopped near the cave entrance. He turned around and looked amused as I climbed up near him. As I stood up, I could see the flicker of a light coming from inside the cave.

"In here," he croaked.

He hopped inside the cave, but I hesitated. This had to be the tomb he was talking about. I continued following him while holding Lion tightly. We passed a couple of torches on the walls as we worked our way deeper inside the cave until we reached a large cavern. There were torches around the inside of the cavern causing dancing shadows around the shapes inside.

Gradually my eyes adjusted, and I could make out different things. In the center of the cavern was a large bed made up of shiny satin sheets and a fluffy pillow. Next to the bed was a table with an unlit candle, several stacked boxes, and an aerosol can.

The vulture coughed a couple of times and then spoke, "This is really the best setup you can have for your body after you die."

He rested one of his wings on the bed.

"A comfortable bed for your body to lie on." Then he wobbled over to the table.

"A candle and matches .... and some cans of food for you to eat. Your body will probably be famished."

Then he glanced at the aerosol can.

"And bug spray. You can't forget the bug spray. No telling how long you will have been lying there."

I was astonished. "What is all this for?" I asked.

"For after you die someday. For when you come back to life of course. It's actually a very comfortable tomb, guaranteed to keep your body in great shape."

"Body?" I asked.

"Yes, and have I ever got a deal for you," he continued, "all of this for just 20 gold coins."

He wanted money?

"Of course, I'll throw in a ceremony and I will cover the entrance of the tomb real well to make sure nobody comes in and disturbs your body."

"My body?" I asked.

"Yes! You know, for when you die. You get all this for just 20 gold coins. Everything you need for when your body comes back to life."

Comes back to life? He's talking about my body reanimating after it has died.

"You do know about coming back to life?" he asked, "It's really a sweet deal."

I looked around the cavern. It, no doubt, was set up for someone waking after dying. This was disturbing. A talking vulture selling a tomb for someone's body to wake up from being dead. It didn't add up.

"I don't know," I said.

"What don't you know? It seems rather simple to me."

He added, "And you know you can trust me.... I have references."

"I just don't know," I said.

"Hold on a second," he replied.

He briefly paused.

"You do believe, don't you?"

"Believe what?"

"That you will come back to life?"

"I'm not sure."

"Oh," he scoffed, "that changes everything."

"What do you mean?"

He raised his large black wings over his head.

"I mean...if you don't believe that you'll come back to life, then you won't come back to life!"

I thought and then I spoke quietly, "That hardly seems fair."

"Well," he started nodding his head in exaggeration, "that's the way it goes!"

We stood in the cavern facing each other for what seemed like several minutes.

I broke the silence, "I think I should go."

"Yes...I think that you should," he agreed.

He turned his back to me as I walked down the torch-lit corridor out to the entrance of the cavern.

So absurd I thought.

I hiked down the mountain and then looked back up. The cavern entrance was gone, and a large bird flew in lazy circles in the sky way above me.

What a day I thought, as I continued hiking hoping to find my way back home.

Devil in the Forest

A fear so deep that seared my core,
the demon shrieked cross forest's floor,
about true terror, this shriek would teach.
What manner of ghoul would use this speech —
a hungry witch is what I swore.

A sound so evil through darkness tore,
visions of monsters, death, and gore.
Take me far from this creature's reach.
A fear so deep.

Would that I could run through a door,
or fly away on wings I wore.
Into my soul the dread would reach,
the first time I heard an owl screech,
walking thru woods, this grisly chore.
A fear so deep

At last

strewn flat across the grassy ground
dead cannonballs of dullish black
now, never into bodies pound
no thudding thuds with sickening cracks

their purpose lost with no attack
now hidden here without a sound
no human fodder left to smack
forgotten missiles, smooth and round

but now amongst the orbs are found
this beauty from a fallen stack
around a round gently wound
two white tulips back-to-back

Angel 4

I stopped walking after a while and began to wonder. Is this what Boris wanted me to do? I lay down and after a few minutes, fell asleep. And I dreamed of a great war with tanks, jets, and bombs. I heard gunfire with a steady rap rap rap.

Suddenly, I heard someone clear their throat.

"Ahem."

I jumped up and scrambled to focus on the figure standing in front of me. I grabbed Lion and held him tight.

In front of me was a tall man in a green dress uniform and a green beret. He was standing straight up. His uniform had three gold stars on both shoulders, and he had medals and ribbons across the front of his jacket. He even had a couple of medals on his pants leg. He was clean-shaven with steel-blue eyes and a jutting jaw. He was not smiling.

Wow, I thought.

"Can I help you?" I spoke.

"Sir," he said.

"Yes?" I asked.

"I would like you to address me as sir."

"Oh okay..... sir."

I felt a little annoyed. Now, what was this about?

"I heard you are a writer," he said.

"Well, evidently that's what some people think," I answered, thinking of Boris.

"Sir," he said.

"Sir," I repeated.

"Fine, then you shall be my scribe."

"Scribe?........ Sir?" I remembered.

"Yes! You will follow me around and write of my exploits as I conquer the world."

Ok. This guy is telling me he wants to conquer the world. Something told me I should be very careful dealing with him. I leaned to the side to look behind him. There was nobody.

"And how will you do this?" I quizzed.

"Sir," he said

"Sir," I answered

"I will raise a great army. Then I will sweep across the globe conquering all in my path."

This didn't sound too good.

He continued, "And you shall be my scribe."

He smiled, "I will be immortal."

I stood still.

"I will be famous for all time. People will read about me throughout eternity. I will be remembered by all."

He spoke again as he looked serious, "And after all, to be held in the minds of humanity forever, well, isn't that the same as living forever?"

I paused long enough to ponder what he was saying. He posed an interesting question. Some might say that to be in the memories of all might be close to being alive. But forever? That seemed preposterous.

"First of all, sir," I said, "I don't think I would make a very good scribe. I'm actually kind of a beginner when it comes to writing."

"Second thing, sir," I continued, "I don't agree that conquering the world would keep you famous forever. I mean, in ten thousand years, you may be barely a footnote."

He seemed to be getting annoyed.

"And," I added, "the world will disappear someday. There won't be anyone left to remember you."

"Aha!" he said, "What about space travel and colonizing the planets? That would extend humanity and their memory of me forever."

This was getting out of hand. I wondered, should I explain to him that the solar system, the galaxy, and even the known universe is temporal?

"I got you there!" he trumpeted.

He smiled at me. Then his smile turned serious.

"Maybe you're right about not being my scribe," he said. "I'll bet I could do better with someone who had a little more faith."

With that, he turned around and marched away. I watched until he was out of sight and looked down at Lion.

"What do you think boy? What's going on here?"

I looked around. The area still didn't look familiar. I was lost. And I was bumping into a lot of questionable characters. Oh well, I thought and started walking again.

the hunter

moments before,
by cause of a startling piece of metal
stinging through the neck,
the eerie death bawl of a deer
echoing,
this beauty fallen
on crunchy needles of pine.

approaching steps, snapping,
first far, then near,
to a final stillness,
as the misting snorts of blood
pulse out and in a moment —
slow,
and stop.

standing legs covered in britches
with streaks of green and olive
above brown rubber boots
hold with silence —
then to the earth on knees
with shaking hands cupping his face —
oh, the raucous sobbing.

Angel 5

I continued walking. I could tell Lion was getting tired. As I held him in my arms, his head would bob with each step. He was having a hard time keeping his small black eyes open. If only I could remember my way through this desert.

That's when I saw the fire. A four-foot cactus was in flames in the middle of the desert.

I set Lion on the ground, scooped up a handful of sand in my hands, and ran over to the burning cactus. Then the moment before I threw the sand at the fire, a voice arose from within the flames.

"Excuse me," said the burning cactus.

I stood up, dropping the handful of sand onto the ground.

"That's better," said the deep voice from within the flames.

I stood silent. Now what!

While the fire continued burning, the cactus in the middle showed no sign of being burnt.

I stood looking at the flames and said nothing. After a few minutes, I finally spoke.

"And who are you?"

There was a pause and then the fire spoke.

"I am the protector of this cactus."

"Angel," said Lion sitting behind me.

My head spun around, and I looked at my small terrier sitting on the ground. He just looked back at me.

"Did you say something, Lion?" I asked.

No answer.

"Say something."

No answer.

I turned my attention back to the flames.

"Did you do that?" I asked the fire.

No answer.

This did not sit well with me. My little dog, my partner for years, spoke. I had a sinking feeling in my stomach.

"Please don't mess with my dog," I said.

"Are you here to touch this cactus?" asked the flaming cactus, showing no signs of flaming out.

"No...I don't usually touch a cactus."

"Ahhh..." it said, "but this is a very special cactus."

I was still annoyed about Lion talking.

"Do you want to live forever?" asked the cactus that was on fire.

The question struck me as having to do with everything I had experienced up to this point. First, there was the parrot. He was trying to extend his life, if not find immortality. Then there was the vulture. He seemed to think that if I believed that I would come back to life after I died, then that indeed was what would happen. And thirdly was the unstable general. He seemed to think that if he could live in the minds of people forever, it would be the same as living forever.

They all were trying to be immortal in their own unique way. But this fire, or angel, as Lion called it, seemed somehow to connect touching the cactus with immortality. Maybe that's why it was guarding the cactus with fire.

"Most beings would love to be immortal," added the fire.

"Yes...I see that. I have met some of them," I answered.

"Well?"

"Well, what?" I answered.

"Are you here because you want immortality?"

I thought a second.

"I don't think I really want to live forever. I'm not sure why. But no, I don't want to be immortal."

"So, why are you here?" queried the burning cactus.

"Well, I am trying to get home...you see... I ran into this angel named Boris, a strange fellow... and..."

"Oh, Boris!" the flames exclaimed, "I know Boris." The flames leaped a couple of feet higher.

"Yes..." I continued, "you see Boris gave me some kind of mission that I'm not sure about and..."

I paused for a moment.

"Look, I just want to get home."

"Me too," said Lion.

I looked Lion right in the eyes.

I looked back at the cactus.

"I wish you would stop that," I said to the fiery cactus. I was getting very frustrated. Exasperated, I spoke again.

"This has got to be a dream."

That's when the burning cactus made a comment that sounded almost like a riddle, "A dream is only a dream...after you awaken."

"Huh?" I said.

The flames jumped into the air and could feel the heat on my face. I backed up a couple of steps and scooped up Lion.

The fire settled a bit and then it spoke again.

"Do you want to wake up?"

I didn't know what to say so I didn't say anything.

"Go find Dwayne," the fire said as if I knew who Dwayne was.

"Who's Dwayne?" I asked.

"Dwayne knows the secret of life. Dwayne can awaken you."

At this point, I really didn't want to know the secret of life. I just wanted to go home and find out what was wrong with my dog.

"Where is Dwayne?" I asked.

"Any direction," the fire answered, "He is in any direction you go. Just walk and you will find him."

I shrugged and decided to leave. I'd had enough. I suppose Lion's talking had put me in a not-so-good mood. I turned and walked away from the burning cactus.

After a few minutes of walking while holding Lion in my

arms, I looked back and could see a column of smoke rising far off behind me. I turned and continued walking, occasionally looking at Lion and asking him if he had anything to say.

He said nothing.

urgent

fight then fight
against the wind
struggle then struggle
with mission and purpose
to press for advantage

reaching, desiring, believing
that life without ambition
is a breathless, lifeless
corpse having betrayed birth
itself

but be it in the light
of the greatest star or in
the darkness of the deepest hole
the striver
knows no peace

Prior to Eternity

remember when we all could see,
prior to eternity,
we laid in glades on silky dew,
peeked thru branches, jigsaws of blue,
touched close the heartbeat of a tree,

we'd skim the surges of the sea,
and swim the skies, stretched and free,
soar thru valleys of greenish hue,
remember when.

slept 'neath the stars, heaven's marquee,
prior to eternity,
brooks melodies we'd nestle to,
crunchy brown leaves we'd scamper thru,
every breath, an act of beauty,
remember when.

Angel 6

As I walked while carrying Lion, I wondered what else was going to happen. It didn't take long for me to find out. I stopped and looked in front of me at something very puzzling.

A large tortoise was on what looked like a stone in the middle of a clearing. Just in front of him was a blueish ribbon stretched across the clearing, tied on either end to scrub bushes. But the strangest sight was that the tortoise was wearing little red sneakers on each of his stubby feet. They were roundish and were tied to the top.

It was all I could do to keep from laughing. I gulped to stay collected and looked down at him. He slowly raised his head and looked at both Lion and me.

"Howdy," he said with a slow drawl.

"Hi," I said. I seemed to be taking this new situation all in stride. These encounters were not surprising to me much anymore.

"My name is Dwayne," he said slowly with a definite southern accent.

"Hi, Dwayne," I said, "I was told I would meet you."

"Well, I declare...." he said, "... y'all are in the right place then...so y'all want to talk to me?"

"Yes, I think so."

"Sho Nuff..." he answered, "...now what can I do fer you?"

I thought for a second. What would he say if I told him about the talking cactus?

I quickly dismissed this thought. It was probably all in a day for him.

"A flaming cactus told me you would give me the secret to life," I said.

He stuck his round head way out of the large shell and began looking me up and down as if he were measuring me in some way. After a minute he relaxed and seemed satisfied with me.

"Yah...reckon I can help you with that."

He slowly waddled closer to me. It seemed like the tiny sneakers made it harder for him to crawl.

"I had a vision once," he said as he looked into my eyes, "Y'all understand what I'm saying there?"

"I think so," I said.

"Bless your heart.... now you understand that I'm fixin' to show you the answer to all your problems?"

"Yes," I nodded.

This was getting interesting. Maybe this is what all the nonsense was leading up to.

He continued.

"Here it is. Life is a horserace...and everyone is trying to get ahead.... you follow?"

"I follow," I answered.

I felt a little strange saying that, but I understood what he was saying. Among people, it sure seemed like a grand competition. Even among animals and plants, life seemed to be constantly competing.

He suddenly looked very serious, or as serious as a tortoise wearing sneakers can look.

"The secret to life," he said, "is that you are already ahead!"

I stood silent as I let that sink in.

"You don't have to try to be on top. You already are!" he added.

I began to feel a little strange as he continued.

"You don't need to race, partner.........you've already won!"

I began to feel a little dizzy. Then Lion spoke up.

"I get it!"

"Huh?" I looked down at Lion.

"Y'all follow me.... don't ya?" said the tortoise.

"Do you follow me?" asked Lion.

What was going on? I felt very strange. It was as if I could see things more clearly, yet it seemed like a thin veil covered me.

"I get it. I get it," said Lion.

All at once, I seemed to be able to evaluate things more

purposely. I had more choices. But at the same time, I felt less alive. It was hard to understand.

"I'm getting tired of this desert," complained Lion.

"It's a horse race.... and you are already ahead of everyone!" drawled the tortoise.

"When am I going to eat?" asked Lion.

Suddenly, Lion was very talkative. I looked at the tortoise and asked, "Are you the one saying the words my dog seems to be speaking?"

Lion continued, "I remember when I was just a puppy. I was a very fast runner."

I glared at Lion as he continued talking.

"God, I can be stupid sometimes," Lion said.

"What?" I said in disbelief.

Then the Tortoise spoke to me, "Now you are plumb enlightened."

"Did I do something wrong?" asked Lion.

The tortoise continued, "So now it's time for you to do your duty."

"It's very dry out here," said Lion.

"My duty?" I asked.

"Yes, your duty to the world, to help humanity."

This was getting a little complicated. Maybe he was right. Maybe it was time for me to help the world.

"And how do I do that?" I asked.

"Here...kitty...kitty...kitty..." said Lion.

"You must find the four Gifted Ones...and I reckon you can then figure out which gift you want to have."

"Oh," I said.

"It sure has been a long day," said Lion.

"And where do I find these Gifted Ones?" I asked.

"No worries you will find them," the tortoise said.

"I'm not fond of poodles.... they smell," spoke Lion.

"And would you please stop saying those things through my dog!" I said with some sternness.

"Now don't have a hissy fit. If your dog is talking, I shore enuff can't hear it," answered the tortoise.

With that, he slowly waddled down the path and eventually disappeared behind a mesquite bush.

"Well, he's a cheery fellow," quipped Lion.

"Could you just be quiet for a minute?" I said to Lion.

I looked around. It was getting dark, and I had no idea what to do next.

Lion continued to chatter. It almost felt as though Lion was my conscience. Whatever he was spouting, it sure seemed like he was doing a lot of judging. I sat down and thought about the day. My head was swimming, and I had no idea why. Maybe, as Dwayne insinuated, I would find my calling with a gifted one and I would understand better what was happening.

As the night went on, Lion finally stopped talking. It was getting cold. It can get surprisingly cold in the desert. I lay down and cuddled with Lion to keep us both warm. In the quiet of the desert, I fell asleep.

dabbing

who invented the small sponge-on-a-stick?
maybe someone with compassion
and sorrow in their heart.

a touch of water — a dabbing — is traced
across a gaping mouth
like ice on a lingering burn.

this ritual of mercy,
this comforting, ended
with empty beds sadly neat.

but often this moistness was gifted
by a dabber unknown to the
still ones.

as abandoned they were
by the pious who declared
the deaths were deserved.

and so I am grateful
for the love of the builder
of the sponge-on-a-stick.

names

block longhand stencil
sewn bright
these panels
linen cotton silk
stretched across the king's lawn
with soft billows
whispering in colors
goodbye

Angel 7

"Are you looking for the healer?"

I opened my eyes and jumped to a sitting position. It was morning and there in front of me was a roadrunner balancing on one leg with the other leg bent to the side in an awkward way.

"Oh, oh," said Lion.

I rubbed my eyes and looked at the bird with its bright red streak alongside its head and its black and white speckled feathers.

"Are you talking to me?" I asked.

"Yes, I am in need of the gifted one, the healer," the roadrunner spoke, "Do you know where I can find her?"

I remembered what Dwayne the tortoise had said and then answered the roadrunner.

"I think I am looking for her too."

"Of course you are," said Lion.

I wished at that moment that Lion would just be quiet.

"Well then," said the roadrunner, "we should look together."

"Ok," I said

With that, the roadrunner began to hop in a direction towards the morning sun. It wasn't difficult to follow as it couldn't go very fast on one foot.

"I don't trust him," said Lion.

I just tried to ignore Lion. Since he started talking after I met Dwayne, I had difficulty focusing on what I was doing. It was very distracting and, at times, difficult to ignore.

We followed the roadrunner around a few mesquite bushes and over a large flat rock when he suddenly stopped hopping.

"There she is!" said the roadrunner.

I looked ahead of him and saw a woman dressed in a white robe that went down to her feet. She had a white squarish hat on and a white face mask over her mouth and nose with thin straps running behind her head under a white veil covering the back of her head. Even from the short distance I was away from her, I could see that she had piercing green eyes.

In front of her, facing her, was a short line of three animals. The first was a silvery lynx with one of its eyes half shut. Behind the lynx was a coyote that looked like it was missing one ear and behind the coyote was a large rabbit who seemed to wheeze with each breath from his small nose.

"Now that's a motley crew," said Lion.

"Please be quiet," I said back to him.

The woman in white continued facing the lynx and the line behind it as the roadrunner hopped to the back of the line behind the rabbit. I walked up beside her.

"Hello," I said.

She glanced at me and spoke back to me in a very pleasant voice, "Hello."

She turned back to the line of animals and focused on the lynx. She then placed her hand over the lynx's half-closed eye and whispered something.

The lynx jumped up and then fell over and lie on the ground for a few moments. It slowly got up and amazingly, both of the lynx's eyes looked normal.

"Holy cow!" said Lion.

The lynx then began thanking the woman profusely.

She smiled at the large cat and said, "You are very welcome. I am very glad to be of service."

I was wowed. This was one of the gifted ones. She was gifted with the ability to heal others. How wonderful that must be! Maybe what Dwayne was saying was that I too could be a healer.

"Excuse me," I said to the healer as the lynx bound away.

She turned to me. I could feel her smile even though I could not see it through her white face mask.

"You just healed that lynx!" I spoke.

"Yes," she answered.

"This whole thing looks disorganized," said Lion.

"I apologize for my dog's comments. I don't know what's gotten into him."

"I didn't hear anything from your dog," she stated.

Weird, I thought. Then my mind went back to her incredible healing of the eye of the lynx.

"How did you do that?" I asked.

"It's a gift," she said while smiling. She then turned her attention to the eagerly awaiting one-eared coyote.

She placed her hand over the missing ear and whispered something to the other ear. She then removed her hand, and the coyote had an ear where there was none before. I was astounded.

The coyote bowed to her and then ran off out of sight.

"That was incredible!" I exclaimed.

"Thank you," she said.

Maybe I could do this. Maybe I could somehow get the gift of healing others. I felt like maybe this was what all these encounters were leading to.

Next was the wheezing rabbit who was having problems breathing through its nose. The woman in white covered the rabbit's nose with her hand and whispered to it.

She took her hand away and looked down at the rabbit. But, after a few moments, it was clear the rabbit was still having problems breathing.

She again put her hand over the rabbit's nose and this time loudly spoke.

"Heal!"

She took her hand away and again, after a few moments, the rabbit continued to wheeze.

I was disappointed.

"What happened?" I asked her.

She looked over at me and in a calm voice said, "It was because of him. He didn't believe enough, so he wasn't healed."

The rabbit shook its head and slowly hopped away. I could hear the wheezing slowly disappear as the rabbit moved away.

"You mean it was his fault that he wasn't healed?" I asked.

"I'm hungry," said Lion.

She then turned her attention to the roadrunner without answering me.

Something struck me as not right. On one hand, it was the healer who was healing these animals. But on the other hand, if they were not healed, it was their fault, not the healer's.

I turned around and slowly walked away as she started to bend over to the roadrunner. I'm not sure why, but I had lost the desire to be a healer.

As I got further away, I felt sorry for the rabbit. It was bad enough that he had a breathing problem. But now he felt it was his fault for having the problem.

It was time for me to look for a different gifted one.

hidden hearts

at times
hearts are like diamonds,
unseen,
hidden deep in caves
of fear —
among the safety
of dark boulders

but when the starlight
sneaks
past a crevice,
thru the dusty air,
across the scattered floor,
the diamonds gleam,
radiant,
in the light of grace

I am them

I look at the trees
shaking at the clouds
while beneath,
rabbits and foxes
play hide-and-seek

and soaring ravens
scream hidden omens
as lazy minnows in the shallows
kiss the surface
making gentle circles

and I am them,
just dust clumped together
with the light of
a billion stars
peering out

Angel 8

I walked for a while as the sun rose higher in the sky. It might be getting hot soon, I thought. I wanted to find my cabin.

As I came into a small canyon, I looked down and saw another strange sight. It was a thin man in a spiffy black tuxedo. He was wearing white gloves, waving his hands around and mumbling unintelligible words. He also had a hat and was pulling things out of it that looked like they couldn't fit.

"Oh great, now what?" complained Lion.

I walked up beside the formally dressed man and said, "Hi."

He became startled and turned to face me. He looked to be about 30 years old and wore round spectacles.

"Well, hello," he said, "It is my pleasure to meet you this fine day."

I smiled. He seemed to be very nice.

"Hi," I answered, "We are looking for a gifted one. We were sent by Dwayne. Are you a gifted one?"

He laughed.

"Some say I am. I, sir, am a magician. Some say I work miracles."

"Of course," he added, "That would depend on how you were

brought up. Some people believe in magic and some believe in miracles. And some believe in both."

"Wow," I said.

"Wow," Lion said.

The magician bowed, "Happy to be of service."

I thought for a second. This could be my destiny. I always loved watching magicians when I was a child.

"What kind of magic?" I asked.

"I manifest things...I make things come into existence you might say."

This was very interesting. I could see myself becoming a magician. How great it must be to do magic.... or miracles.

"Can you show me?" I asked somewhat sheepishly.

"Well..." He reached behind his shirt at his neck and showed me a large gold chain that was hanging around his neck.

"How about this?" he said as he released it back under his white shirt.

"I want one of those," said Lion.

"Please be quiet," I said.

"Well, you're the one who asked me," spoke the magician.

"Oh, I'm sorry...I was talking to my dog. He keeps interrupting me. It's very distracting."

"I didn't hear your dog say anything," said the magician.

I realized at that moment that only I could hear my dog's meandering speech. I just had to learn to try and ignore him. I wondered for a second if maybe Lion's words were from me. I dismissed it.

"That's a very nice gold chain," I said bringing the conversation back to his magic.

"Yep," he said, "solid gold.... I manifested it. I made it appear into my life."

"That looks very valuable," I said. I was genuinely impressed.

"I also manifested you," he said, "Another miracle."

"Me?" I asked.

"Yep, I asked the Universe for someone to mentor...someone to teach my magic to, and well, here you are."

His magic abilities could be a gift that would be very useful, I thought. The skill to manifest or create anything in one's life would be awesome.

"This is pretty wild," said Lion.

I ignored Lion and spoke to the magician.

"Can you show me how I can make things appear in my life?"

"I sure can," he said.

He waved his hand in the air, made a fist, and with the other hand pulled an endless length of colorful scarves from his fist. He then bent over and looked both ways and then whispered to me.

"All you have to do is ask the Universe for whatever you want....and then thank the Universe for giving it to you."

"You mean thank the Universe even if I haven't gotten anything?" I asked.

"No, no, no," he answered, "you have to believe that you already have it. Only then will you get it."

"Oh."

"Yes...you see...if you have any thoughts that say you don't have it, then it won't happen."

He looked at the puzzled look on my face.

"Ok...let's try it. What is it that you want more than anything?"

I paused and wondered and then I realized what I wanted.

"I want to go home to my cabin."

"Me too," said Lion.

"Ok," said the magician, "now simply believe that you are home at your cabin and then the Universe will give your wish to you."

I closed my eyes and tried believing that I was already home. After a few moments I opened my eyes, and I was in the same spot holding Lion while standing in front of the magician. I was still lost in the desert.

"We're not home," said Lion.

I looked at the magician with a confused look.

"It didn't work," I said.

"Did you believe that you were already home?"

"I thought I did. Maybe if I start walking, it will happen."

"All you have to do is know that it has already happened. You don't need to do anything else. You may just need to give it a little more time."

"This doesn't make any sense," said Lion.

I looked down at the ground. Lion was right. This did not make much sense.

"You know," I said, "I think I'll try and find my cabin by walking."

"Oh," said the magician. "ok, suit yourself."

With that, he turned his back to me and began waving his hands in the air. He must have been manifesting something, I thought. I slowly walked away wondering if I had done something wrong.

a dream

Island Island

a firm lump of land
cryptic tongues we could not

understand

past the glass
a truck marked U.S. did not belong

the smell of war was very strong

buying in secret all the food
hiding in earnest their fearful mood

time to go
Time to Leave

but the air was slammed SHUT

atom rockets,
* they may fly,*
*   back and forth,*
*   across the sky,*

they Knew

Angel 9

I walked for a long time, stopping every so often to close my eyes and try to manifest my cabin. But nothing happened.

Then as I walked up over a rise, I came face to face with a seated woman in a colorful skirt and shirt with bright scarves wrapped around her neck. On her head was a bright yellow bandana. She was middle-aged with heavy eye makeup and bright red lipstick. In front of her was a large crystal ball that she was gazing at with her hands suspended a few inches above it.

"Hi," I spoke.

She looked up at me and whispered, "Shhhh!"

I did not say anything as she looked back down at the crystal ball and started humming.

"Now what!" exclaimed Lion.

After a few more moments she looked back at me and placed her hands in her lap.

"Do you want a reading?" she asked in a gruff voice.

"I'm not sure," I said, "Are you a gifted one?"

"Yes...I tell futures," she answered.

"Wow," said Lion.

Now, this was something I would love to do, I thought. To

know the future would be a gift that I could truly use. But like the last two gifted ones, maybe there was a catch to this.

"How do you do that?" I asked.

"Well," she said, "telling futures is also called reading. And that's what I do. I read."

"Read?" I asked

"Yes, read. I take in all the hints...the signs...the obvious...and I put it all together and then predict. These signs come from observation and listening. You might even say they are given to me."

"Give me a break," said Lion.

"Given?" I asked.

"Yes.... given from the person or place I am reading for or given from a divine source, whichever you prefer to call it."

"And your predictions always come true?" I asked

"Well, that part needs a little explaining. You see, it depends on if it's bad news or good news and if the person who hears the prediction believes in it."

"Wacky, I tell you," said Lion.

I tuned Lion out and asked her to explain, "How's that?"

"You see if I told a squirrel he was going to fall out of a tree and hurt himself badly and he believed the prophecy, what would he then do?"

I thought a second.

"I think he may not climb any trees."

"Exactly," she said, "and that would mean the prophecy was wrong."

"I see," I said thoughtfully.

"But," she continued, "if the prediction was good...let's say...I predict you are going to meet the love of your life soon, you would then be on the lookout for this new love and may grasp at the first sign of compatibility which may turn out not to be the love of your life."

"Oh," I said a bit confused.

She saw my confusion.

"What I am trying to say is that if the person believes in the prediction, they will do something to affect the result thereby making the prediction null and void. The prediction then becomes a sort of suggestion."

"Oh. I get it. But what if the person doesn't believe the prediction?"

"That, my friend, is the sweet spot. If you make a prediction and they don't believe it...and it comes true...then you have made a true prophecy."

My head was starting to spin. There were so many rules to predicting.

"So, you see," she continued, "the only real prediction is the prediction you make to somebody who doesn't believe you can see into the future."

I must have looked confused again as I turned over in my mind what she had just said. Then I had a thought.

"What if they don't believe you, the prediction comes true, and they think it was just luck?"

She looked both ways and leaned over to me and whispered, "Then they'd be right."

I stepped back surprised. My shock then turned to disappointment. So now she was saying that if a prediction was true, it was just luck? This did not feel right at all.

"Quack! Quack!" yelled Lion.

I decided then that this was not for me.

She watched my reaction and then closed her eyes. She mumbled some words that I couldn't hear and then held the back of her hand against her forehead and started droning in a low voice.

She opened her eyes, looked at me, and said, "I predict you will be leaving soon."

I thought for a second about staying just to prove her wrong but decided against it. I turned while holding Lion and slowly walked away.

Her prediction was right this time, but I still didn't believe she could tell the future. She was just lucky on this one.

Teaching

Do not tell me where
the emptiness is
as I might worship
your words

Do not tell me that
you hold the secrets
as I might worship
you

Please just give me
hints so that
my heart may
find the moment

Angel 10

So, we continued moving through the prickly brush and rocks of the desert heading towards what I had hoped would be the cabin that was my home. As I walked, I wondered if I would bump into the fourth and last gifted one. I only had one more chance. I had no desire to embrace the gifts of the first three, so this next one had to be it.

Did I have to be gifted if I was enlightened? Was I really enlightened? I was beginning to doubt what the tortoise had told me. Was I ahead of everyone else? Did I believe I was ahead of everyone else?

Maybe the point was to stop striving to be ahead. But there was something that didn't sit right with me putting myself as a winner above others.

Lion would occasionally break out in nonsensical chatter as I carried him. A lot of times he seemed to be judging or criticizing others and, even at times, criticizing me. I missed the times when he would just look at me and speak with his eyes telling me that he was content.

Then I stopped near a Joshua tree. Perched on a branch about three feet above me was a large gray owl. He was looking down at me with very large eyes. On top of his head was a small, black mortarboard, much like the mortarboard caps that graduates wear at graduation ceremonies. Hanging along the side was a gold tassel. This sight was a little absurd.

"Hello," he said.

"Hello," said Lion.

I waited to hear him respond to Lion.

"Hello," the owl said again.

I continued to look at him and realized that I had forgotten that only I could hear Lion speak.

"Hello?" the owl said.

"Hello," I said, "Who are you?"

"My, we are a little aggressive, aren't we?" he said.

"What do you mean?" I asked.

"You said hoo. Now, you are clearly not an owl. That is species appropriation."

"I'm sorry...Ummm...what do they call you?"

He had tilted his head down a little and the gold tassel fell between his eyes. He harrumphed and snapped his head, so the tassel swung back up and off to the side.

"I am Owl," he said, "I am a teacher."

"Oh," I said intrigued, "are you a gifted one?'

"You may say that."

"What do you teach?"

"I teach everything."

"Who do you teach?"

"That's enough of that!" he snapped.

"Oh, please," said Lion.

"Sorry," I said.

He then bent his head down and the gold tassel fell between his eyes again. He snapped his head so the tassel swung back up and off to the side and glared at me.

It struck me that maybe this was my destiny. I loved to learn so I probably would love to teach. After all, isn't teaching the prize for learning?

"Can you teach me how to teach?"

He looked back down at me. I was waiting for his tassel to fall across his eyes again.

"Are you competent at expiscation?" he asked

"Huh?" I asked.

"I get that when my stomach gets upset," said Lion.

Owl sighed. "Research...investigation," he said.

"Oh. I think so," I answered slightly embarrassed.

"Well." he said thoughtfully, "I am well versed in andragogy."

I stayed silent. I did not want Owl to find out that I didn't know what andragogy meant.

"...and I am polyhistor..." he continued.

This time Lion was silent with me.

"...so, adjure me anything."

I was impressed. Owl certainly could teach me a lot. And then I could be a teacher just like Owl.

"I don't know what you said but I would love to learn from you," I said.

Owl slowly turned his head 360 degrees around and then looked at me sharply.

"Will you do anything I say?"

"Yes," I answered.

"Yes," Lion answered.

"Fine," said Owl, "then you can be my student-ee."

That was kind of strange.

"Do you mean student?" I asked.

Owl turned his head back 360 degrees.

"Umm.... well.... what do you think I meant?" he said.

"Student," I said.

"If I meant student, then I would have said student!" Owl exclaimed, "No...this is a new word that I made that means a diligent student."

I was confused.

"You need to learn who is the student-ee and who is the teacher here...you need to have beginner's mind...do you follow me?" Owl continued.

I felt doubt creeping into my mind along with a sinking feeling. Is a teacher always right? Do they admit mistakes? Maybe teaching wasn't for me. Or maybe this was the wrong teacher.

I looked at him as he glared at me, occasionally blinking his large eyes. He was waiting for an answer. But I had no idea what to say.

I decided that it was time to leave.

I looked at Owl and spoke, "I have to get going-ee."

I turned around with Lion in my arms and walked away. After a minute of walking, I heard Owl in the distance shout, "I'm going to have to flunk you!"

"Who cares," said Lion.

I didn't care.

But I did become depressed. I could not find my home and I seemed to have reached the end of Boris's mission without an answer for why I was given the mission in the first place.

I think Lion could tell I was depressed. He had stopped chattering.

I just kept walking with my head down.

What do I do now?

Naked

I have put my words there.
My nakedness in the arena.
I see faces.
But I cannot see their thoughts
or hearts.
I only know that they have seen me
and watched my tears.

And now I cannot hide
in this circle of dust.
Are they laughing or sighing?
Do they see me
or do they see themselves?
It is my fault
for becoming bare

Gift 1

So, the walking continued.

I wondered what all these experiences were about. I was not striving for immortality, as some of the encounters seemed to refer. And then I was told by Dwayne that the secret to life was to know that you are already ahead of others. I guess this was so as to not strive or compete with others. And by believing this, I was supposed to find one of the four gifts.

But none of the gifts worked for me.

And it just somehow didn't seem right. To begin with, after listening to Dwayne, I did seem to be more aware. But at the same time, I felt removed. It was almost like I was sleepwalking. And to top it off, that's when Lion began chattering like a self-centered school child.

I felt disappointed. Dwayne was wrong. Putting myself above others was not good. It caused a barrier of sorts.

At least Lion was quiet.

That's when I saw him. He was a tall man, with shoulder-length white hair, all mussed up. He was wearing tennis shoes, jeans, and a dirty t-shirt. He had a small, tattered, backpack on his back and looked like he had not had a bath in ages. Around his neck was an old string that was attached to a worn-down pencil hanging down in front of him.

Something seemed off although I couldn't quite put my finger on it. He was partially bent at the waist and was looking at the desert floor. His lips were moving, and it appeared he was counting. Maybe he was counting rocks. I had no idea.

I walked up beside him. "Excuse me," I said.

Then he spoke louder but continued looking at the ground.

"...seven-thousand two hundred and twenty-two.... seven-thousand two hundred and twenty-three...."

I touched him on the arm. "Excuse me," I repeated.

He immediately straightened up and without looking at me, placed his hands over his ears and began screaming.

"AHHHH!....AHHHH!......AHHH!"

"Ok, ok.... I'm sorry," I said as I stepped back.

With that, he mumbled something and began counting again. I assumed he was counting rocks.

"seven-thousand two hundred and twenty-six.... seven-thousand two hundred and twenty-seven.... seven-thousand two hundred and twenty-eight...."

I surmised that he was somehow intellectually challenged. Maybe it was autism. Maybe it was delirium. Perhaps he had eaten a peyote button. But any kind of communication was going to be difficult.

"What are you counting?" I asked.

He looked up and his head was moving in motion as if he was watching a fly buzz around his head. "...counting angels.... counting angels.... yes...yes...he's counting angels..." he said.

With that, he began to walk away. His arms stayed at his side as he walked, which looked awkward.

I sped up and began walking next to him. Maybe he was lost just like me.

"Where are you going?" I asked as I walked alongside him.

He stopped and looked up. It was as if he was looking at something above his head.

"Have to go home before dark.... have to go home before dark...feed the doggie...feed the doggie...." he said.

"I'm trying to go home too!" I exclaimed, "Maybe we can help each other."

He then began looking at the non-existent fly buzzing around his head and spoke again.

"...counting angels...counting angels...."

I was a little disheartened. I wasn't sure how to get through to him. And I didn't feel like I could leave him alone.

But there was another thing that was strange. Lion still hadn't said a word. He was quiet. I looked at Lion and spoke "Lion, don't you have something to say?"

Lion just looked at me with his dark round eyes and said nothing.

The man began walking again without moving his arms and he had a slight tilt to his head. Again, I sped up and walked alongside him.

I tried a different approach.

"Do you have a dog too?" I asked.

He stopped and did the follow-the-fly thing with his head again.

".... feed the doggie...feed the doggie...got to feed the

doggie...feed the doggie..." he said rapidly. He then began his march forward again.

As I walked alongside him, I leaned over.

"What kind of dog do you have?" I asked hoping to get a conversation going.

Just then, as I was looking at him as we walked forward, I bumped into the branch of a mesquite bush and scraped my cheek.

"Ouch!" I yelled.

I stopped and felt my cheek. It was bleeding slightly.

He continued walking and was moving away from me. It was frustrating. How could I help him if I couldn't understand what was going on with him?

I ran up to him and began walking alongside him again. I decided to try and see how aware he was.

"Do you know what day it is?" I asked him, not knowing the actual answer myself.

"Gracie, what day is it today?" he said as he walked.

"Huh?" I spoke.

".... well, I don't know," he answered.

He continued walking straight ahead.

"...you can find out if you look at that paper on your desk..." he said.

I wondered who he was talking to.

"...oh, George, that doesn't help. It's yesterday's paper...."

I thought a second. This was some comedy routine he had heard.

"Gracie, what day is it today?" he started again.

"Could you stop for a second?" I asked.

"...well, I don't know..."

"Just stop."

"...you can find out if you look at that paper on your desk..."

I reached out to touch him and get his attention. He stopped and placed his hands over his ears and began screaming like before.

"AHHHH!....AHHHH!....AHHHH!"

I quickly did damage control.

"Look.... look.... I'm sorry...I won't touch you again. Please relax..."

He stopped and then just stood still with his head slightly cocked like he was listening for something.

"Look.... tell me about your doggie...where is he?" I asked.

A light seemed to go on in his eyes. He reached over his shoulder into the small backpack, pulled out an old spiral notebook, and opened it up to an empty page. He then held the notebook just a couple of inches away from his face and with his other hand gripped the small, worn pencil hanging around his neck and began frantically scribbling on the page.

I was surprised. What was this going to be? Maybe a childlike drawing of the desert or maybe his dog.

He was done quickly and ripped the page out of the notebook. He dropped the page and tucked the notebook back in his backpack and began walking again.

I bent over and picked up the page as he walked away. He kept talking.

".... oh, George, that doesn't help. it's yesterday's paper...."

I looked at the page he had dropped and read it:

with all the battle armor
with sharpened weapons
with vigilant guards
posted at each corner
of my soul
how did pint-sized
scruffy dog
covered in matted fur
breach the ramparts
and set up home
in my heart?

It was a poem.

I was in shock. He couldn't carry on a conversation very well but somehow, he could write a decent poem. How could this be? Was he gifted in some way?

I stood for a moment wondering what just happened.

"I saw the angel in the marble and carved until I set him free."
— *Michelangelo*

Gift 2

After reading his poem, I was confounded. Maybe it was just from memory that he wrote or maybe...

I looked down at Lion sitting tucked under my arm. He was quiet, relaxed, and watching everything.

I then ran to catch up to the wandering man. It didn't seem very safe for him to be walking the desert in his state of mind.

When I caught up to him, he was mumbling about counting angels again, and looking around himself. Was he hallucinating?

"That was a nice poem you wrote," I said as we walked.

"...counting angels.... counting angels..." He spoke.

"Do you know any of the gifted ones?" I asked.

He just continued as if he never heard me.

"...counting angels.... counting angels..."

"Where do you see them? What are the angels doing?" I asked.

"...counting angels...counting angels," he continued.

Just as I felt like giving up, he said something different.

"...angels.... everywhere.... everywhere.... everywhere..."

Some acknowledgment.

"What do you mean?" I asked.

".... counting angels.... counting angels....." He was back to counting while looking around. I walked alongside of him for another few minutes holding Lion as he continued counting.

Then I tried a new tact.

"Do you know Dwayne the Tortoise? He told me the secret to life."

With that, he stopped walking. His head began moving in circles as he started mumbling incoherently. I stood next to him, glad that I had gotten his attention.

I looked down at Lion. He was quiet and panting. He had been silent for quite a while now. Maybe he was returning to normal.

I looked back up and the man was now holding his old notebook near his face like before. He raised the worn pencil that was around his neck and began scribbling madly on the page like before.

He stopped as quickly as he had started, ripped the page out of his notebook, and dropped it to the ground. He then began his quick pace away from me.

I picked up the page curious as to what he had written. Maybe it was another poem. I looked at the page and read it:

the race through darkness ends
when leaning over the silent pool
one beholds a reflection
from a thousand pasts

as judgment casts a veil of confusion
and butterflies so faultless
vanish into murky reeds
out of reach

and myriad paths arrest this newfound self
causing choice to mourn for
the purity
of the butterfly

I read through it once and then again. I was shocked. This person had written a visual poem. It was as if this was the way he communicated. I was amazed.

And then it struck me. The poem related to me and my experience. It was a little hard to decipher but it seemed to embody the confusion I'd had ever since learning the 'secret to life.' And the feeling I had from the secret that I had accepted, that seemed to cause the loneliness of self-consciousness, was now gone.

I stared at the poem in amazement. He was no poet laureate, but he definitely could write.

I looked back up and saw that he had walked way ahead of me. I could hear him droning in the distance ".... oh, George, that doesn't help. It's yesterday's paper...."

I held Lion tightly as I began to run to catch up to him. As I was running, I noticed that the rocks and brush that I was passing looked very familiar.

He turned a corner and disappeared out of sight. After a few seconds, I caught up to where he had turned and realized why things seemed familiar.

There, in front of me was my cabin, my home in the desert. I could hardly contain my joy and let out a loud, "Yes!!!"

Lion joined in with a couple of loud barks.

Yes, barks.

I looked down at him. He was a dog again! I was so grateful that he was seemingly back to normal. But somehow, I still felt that his incessant chattering from before had something to do with me.

I then looked all around and could not see the wandering man. Maybe he went into the house.

I was about to walk up to my cabin when I noticed a piece of paper from a spiral notebook lying on the ground. It must be from him, I thought. It was my guess that it was a poem again.

I picked it up and read it:

souls wear the mask of creator
with their crafted notions,
these heaps of lines and circles,
and then in wonder
gaze at the sparkling page.

but know that it is I
who designs —
the unseen heart is my home
and know that when I whisper
that I am Poem.

What did that mean? Was he writing the poem or did the poem miraculously choose him?

I decided not to try and figure it out and ran up to the cabin door and let myself in. I was so relieved that this ordeal was over. I placed Lion on the floor. He promptly ran up to his food bowl and looked at me. I needed to feed him.

I looked throughout the cabin for the wandering man. I decided to look for him again in a few minutes. I was very worried he was still out in the desert.

The scratch on my cheek still hurt and I went into the bathroom to see how bad it was.

That's when I froze.

There I was in the mirror. I had shoulder-length white hair, all mussed up. I was wearing tennis shoes, jeans, and a dirty t-shirt. I had a small, tattered, backpack on my back and looked like I had not had a bath in ages. Around my neck was an old string that was attached to a worn-down pencil hanging down in front of me.

Then I understood.